THIS WALKER BOOK BELONGS TO:

_____

_____

_____

For friends everywhere, especially all my friends
at Beckwithshaw Primary School,
Yorkshire – *P.D.*

For Niamh, Matt, Gabriel and Leo – *N.S.*

First published 2005 by Walker Books Ltd
87 Vauxhall Walk, London SE11 5HJ

This edition published 2006

10 9 8 7 6 5 4 3 2 1

Text © 2005 Penny Dolan
Illustrations © 2005 Nick Sharratt

The right of Penny Dolan and Nick Sharratt to be identified as author and
illustrator respectively of this work has been asserted by them in accordance
with the Copyright, Designs and Patents Act 1988

This book has been typeset in Barmeno

Printed in Singapore

British Library Cataloguing in Publication Data:
a catalogue record for this book is available from the British Library

ISBN-13: 978-0-7445-4066-6
ISBN-10: 0-7445-4066-6

www.walkerbooks.co.uk

Mr Pod
and
Mr Piccalilli

Written by

Penny Dolan and

Nick Sharratt

Illustrated by

Nick Sharratt

WALKER BOOKS
AND SUBSIDIARIES
LONDON · BOSTON · SYDNEY · AUCKLAND

Mr Pod
lived in a first-floor flat.
He lived all alone and
kept himself to himself,
but he did have a cat.

Mr Piccalilli
lived in a ground-floor flat.
He lived all alone and
kept himself to himself,
but he did have a cat.

Mr Pod
called his cat Tod.
Mr Pod loved Tod.

Mr Piccalilli
called his cat Millie.
Mr Piccalilli loved Millie.

One morning
Tod went missing.
Mr Pod searched
high and low...

One morning
Millie went missing.
Mr Piccalilli searched
high and low...

Mr Pod asked at every flat,
but no one had seen Tod.
"Oh dear! Have you seen
my cat, Mr Piccalilli?"
But Mr Piccalilli had not.

Mr Piccalilli asked at every flat,
but no one had seen Millie.
"Oh dear! Have you seen
my cat, Mr Pod?"
But Mr Pod had not.

Mr Pod sat in his flat
and was sad.
Mr Piccalilli must be
feeling sad too,
he thought.

Mr Piccalilli sat in his flat
and was sad.
Mr Pod must be
feeling sad too,
he thought.

Mr Pod
decided to bake
a cheering-up cake
for Mr Piccalilli.

Mr Piccalilli
decided to bake
a cheering-up cake
for Mr Pod.

Mr Pod was carrying
his cake downstairs
when suddenly he heard,
"*Miaow! Miaow! Miaow!*"

Mr Piccalilli was carrying
his cake upstairs
when suddenly he heard,
"*Miaow! Miaow! Miaow!*"

And out of the
landing cupboard
came Tod and Millie
and six little kittens!

Mr Pod and Mr Piccalilli
jumped for joy.
They ate lots of cake
to celebrate.

After that

Mr Pod and Mr Piccalilli

became best friends.

Sometimes Millie and Tod

and the six little kittens

played in Mr Pod's flat.

And sometimes they

played in Mr Piccalilli's flat.

And most times …

everyone was happy!

WALKER BOOKS is the world's leading
independent publisher of children's books.
Working with the best authors and illustrators
we create books for all ages, from babies
to teenagers – books your child will
grow up with and always remember. So…

FOR THE BEST CHILDREN'S BOOKS,
LOOK FOR THE BEAR